TREASURES of CHILD...

W0008489

HATTIE'S SECRET ADVENTURES

BOOK 4 OF
THE HATTIE COLLECTION

Marie Hibma Frost

PUBLISHING
Colorado Springs, Colorado

Hattie's Secret Adventures

Copyright © 1994 by Marie Hibma Frost
All rights reserved. International copyright secured.

Library of Congress Cataloging-in-Publication Data

Published by Focus on the Family Publishing
Colorado Springs, Colorado 80995
Distributed by Word Books, Dallas, Texas

No part of this publication may be reproduced, stored in a retrieval system, or transmitted in any form or by any means—electronic, mechanical, photocopy, recording, or otherwise—without prior permission of the copyright owner.

Editor: Etta Wilson
Interior design: Harriette Bateman
Interior illustration: Buford Winfrey
Cover design: Jeff Stoddard
Cover illustration: Randy Nelson

Printed in the United States of America
94 95 96 97 98 99/10 9 8 7 6 5 4 3 2 1

To my grandchildren,
who encouraged me to tell my stories

Some Words You May Need to Know

bolchey . . . . .junk
dominie . . . . .pastor of a church
ya . . . . .yes
fanka . . . . .little girl
burgermeister . . .mayor

CONTENTS

1. Treasure in the Attic. . . 7

2. Hattie's Crusade against Smoking. . . 15

3. Hattie's Hiding Place. . . 21

4. The Writing Club. . . 29

5. Ruthie on the Roof. . . 35

6. Alone at the Festival. . . 41

7. The Scary Straw Stack. . . 49

8. Tricks. . . 57

9. The Haunted House. . . 65

10. Mary Ann's Mystery. . . 75

11. Dancing with the Mayor. . . 81

12. Easter Joy. . . 89

Chapter 1

Treasure in the Attic

*T*he January day was gray and damp and cold. The Hart children had been playing in the snow for days, and no one wanted to go outside. One Saturday afternoon after they had finished their chores, they couldn't decide what to do.

"We could play house," suggested Hattie.

"I'm tired of playing house," said Clarence.

"Let's make paper dolls from the Sears & Roebuck catalog," Leona offered.

"Dad said we couldn't cut any more pages from the catalog," Hattie reminded her sister.

"Well, we could dress up and act out a play," offered Pierce as he came into the dining room.

"We need extra people to put on a play," answered Hattie, "if it's going to be any good."

"Why not play store?" suggested Mom from the kitchen. "I liked to do that when I was your age."

Mom's idea sounded interesting to Hattie.

"How will we get stuff to sell in our grocery store?" asked Clarence, suddenly interested. "Can we use food from the kitchen?"

"No," laughed Mom. "It doesn't have to be a grocery. Pretend you have a five-and-ten-cent store. That's what we had. We sold a variety of things."

Seeing the look on their faces, Mom continued. "Up in the attic, I have an old wicker basket. It's my *bolchey* basket, but you can take what you want to sell in your play store."

"Can we use anything we find?" asked Hattie.

"Yes, anything from the basket, but nothing else. And nobody should get into my trunk!" warned Mom.

Hattie collected scissors, crayons, and paste and followed everyone up the attic steps. When she got to the top, Pierce had opened the door. Hattie wondered what she would find. The children usually were not allowed in the attic. The room smelled musty and old, and cobwebs hung from the corners. It looked sort of spooky. *Here's a place for adventure!* thought Hattie.

Piles of boxes were stacked against the wall. There was a broken-down chair, a rocker without any rungs, and a cracked mirror leaning against the wall. Leona spied something.

"Here's Mom's *bolchey* basket," said Leona. They all knelt down beside the basket.

"Let's take turns and choose what we want,"

commanded Pierce. "Or Hattie will choose all the good things."

Hattie made a face at him, but she didn't disagree.

"My turn first," said Clarence. He was eyeing an old felt hat with a hole in its top. He could hardly wait to tell the others what he planned to do. "I'll cut off the top and brim," said Clarence, "and I'll have a headband. And I can stick feathers in the band." He held up some colored feathers he had also found in the basket. "Then I'll have an Indian headdress to sell," he said proudly.

"I get to take two things if you do," said Leona. "Else it won't be fair."

She chose a small strip of lace ribbon and a box of buttons of all sizes and shapes. "I'll make these into a necklace if Mom will let me use a needle and thread."

"I'm next," said Hattie, rummaging through the basket. She picked out one white glove. It looked almost new, but had been put with the junk because its mate was missing.

"What are you going to do with just one glove?" asked Clarence.

"Make a puppet," said Hattie knowingly. "I'll use the new box of colored pencils I got for Christmas, and make a face on the tip of each finger and thumb of the glove. Then I'll have a puppet to sell in the store."

"That's pretty clever," admitted Pierce.

Soon everyone was making their gifts for the five-and-ten-cent store. They thought of other things to make too. Leona wanted to braid a belt with some colorful leftover material—but she didn't know how to braid.

Hattie took her hands. "Left side over the middle, right side over the middle, left side over the middle," she said. But Leona's hands were still too little, so Hattie finished it quickly for her.

Pierce framed a picture by using a frame he found in the basket. Clarence found a bag full of cotton and started to stuff it into a ball that wouldn't hold air.

Hattie held on tightly to a small package of loose crystal beads. She couldn't believe Leona hadn't found them. They had once been a crystal necklace, but the string had broken. They were no longer beads, just sparkling crystal jewels. But Hattie couldn't decide what to do with them. Then she looked over at the trunk.

"I wonder if Mom has anything in there I could use?" said Hattie.

Leona looked at Hattie and warned, "I'll tell Mom if you get into her trunk!"

"Mom said don't get *into* the trunk," Hattie quickly answered. "Well, I'm not going to—I wouldn't fit!" she laughed. "I'm just going to open it and look."

"You'll be sorry," said Pierce.

"You'll get us all in trouble," said Clarence.

Hattie nodded her head and went back to making her puppet. But she couldn't resist finding out what was in that trunk. *No harm in looking,* she thought.

In a few minutes everyone else was busy with their own projects. Hattie quietly opened the trunk. There at the very top, she found what she was looking for— a piece of velvet. It was the most beautiful blue she had ever seen. She snatched it from the trunk and closed the lid.

The cloth was in the shape of a triangle. She draped it around her shoulders and it fit just right for a cape. All she would need to do was cut off the points to make it round. Busy with their own projects, the other children didn't see what Hattie was doing.

She tried to cut round corners, but the material was heavy and hard to cut with her blunt scissors. The corners weren't anything like round by the time she finished cutting. *Maybe it will look better when I add the beads,* hoped Hattie. She laid the cloth on the floor and started to glue the crystal beads onto the cloth.

When Hattie finished putting the last bead on the velvet, she picked it up and draped it around her shoulders. She looked at herself in the mirror. She felt positively beautiful! And, oh, how the beads sparkled on the blue velvet!

As she bowed before the mirror, a poem came to mind:

She snatched it from the trunk and closed the lid.

Princess Hattie, how do you do?
You are the prettiest princess I ever knew,
With your hair so gold, and your eyes so blue,
And your cape that sparkles like . . .

Hattie thought hard. *True . . . you . . . new . . . No . . . dew!* That was perfect! *Sparkles like dew!"* she finished.

She twirled around in front of the mirror—right into the arms of Mom, who had come upstairs to see how the children were getting along.

"Hattie! Where did you get that velvet cloth?" asked Mom sternly. "I was saving that piece to make a fancy dress for your doll. You have ruined the material." Mom pointed to the blotches of paste where the beads had fallen off. Hattie hadn't waited for the paste to dry.

"Hattie, take off that velvet and go to your room," Mom ordered.

Hattie left quickly, tears in her eyes. She wouldn't be able to play store with the others. And she wouldn't have a beautiful dress for her doll to wear.

Why is it so hard for me to obey? Hattie asked herself once she was in her room. Dad was always telling her, "Hattie, you have a choice, When you choose not to obey, you have to suffer the consequences."

I certainly suffer a lot of consequences! thought Hattie miserably.

 *Hattie's Crusade against Smoking*

*P*ierce was sitting at the kitchen table, leaning on one elbow, holding his chin. Hattie looked up from the book she was reading and saw the look on his face.

"What's the matter, Pierce? You look like you just lost your best friend."

"I haven't yet, but maybe I will," he replied.

Hattie was puzzled. "What do you mean?" she asked.

"Mr. Van Gelder, our science teacher, told us all about the dangers of smoking last Sunday night."

"Dad smokes," said Hattie, "and he seems okay."

"He seems okay," said Pierce, "but Mr. Van Gelder says smoking could be the death of him."

Hattie was alarmed. Why hadn't she heard about this? She loved Dad and if what Pierce said was true, she had to think of something to keep her dad from dying. All the men at church smoked. Smoking after the service was a Dutch tradition. The men smoked outside while the children were in Sunday school. Maybe they didn't know about the dangers of smoking. Maybe they didn't care!

I'm going to talk to my Sunday school teacher about it, she decided. *He'll be able to help Dad.*

The next Sunday morning, at the beginning of class, Hattie asked her teacher, "Do people die from smoking?"

Mr. Bronkema looked embarrassed. He smoked.

"I suppose it doesn't do anyone any good," he replied. "Maybe we can talk about it some other time."

Hattie wondered why grownups didn't want to answer the really important questions. What was more important than saving her father's life?

That afternoon Hattie thought Pierce might know what to do. "Pierce, help me think of an idea to make Dad quit smoking."

"Oh, Hattie, you don't need any more ideas," Pierce said. "Your ideas always get us in trouble."

Hattie decided she would have to carry on her crusade alone. *I know—I'll hide some of Dad's cigars.* He kept them on a shelf above the stove. Hattie reached for the box. *I'll only take two today and then I'll take some more tomorrow. This way, he won't miss them.*

After she took the cigars, she didn't know what to do with them. Dad never comes in our bedroom. I'll hide them in a dresser drawer. She hurried upstairs to the room she shared with her little sister Leona. She stuck the cigars at the very back of the drawer behind her summer petticoat—the same drawer where Leona kept her clean underwear.

Several days later, Hattie and Leona were in the parlor playing checkers. Dad was reading the paper.

"I must be smoking more than I used to," he said. "My cigars don't seem to last as long."

Leona wrinkled her nose. "Dad, your smoking stinks up the whole house," she said. "Even my petticoat smells like tobacco!"

Hattie turned away to hide her smile. She knew where Dad's cigars were—and why Leona's petticoat smelled!

Dad ignored Leona's remark. Still thinking about his low supply of cigars, he said, "I'll have to get another box when I go to town tomorrow. Then again, maybe I should smoke my pipe more. It's probably cheaper than smoking cigars."

Hattie's heart sank. Her plan wasn't working. Maybe if she did something to the pipe to make it taste bad, Dad would give it up. Soap flakes! That would do it. She put some soap flakes in his pipe and rubbed them around and around with her finger. Then she put the pipe back.

The next time Dad lit up his pipe, he complained, "This tobacco tastes terrible! They must be making bad brands these days! The stuff tastes like soap!" Soon he went back to smoking cigars.

Hattie decided to tell Pierce about her secret plans and how they were not working.

"You'll have to do something more drastic," said Pierce. "Something really slimy that will make the cigars taste real bad."

"Slimy! I know what I'll do," said Hattie. "Thanks for the idea, Pierce."

That Saturday night Hattie slipped to the shed where Dad kept his tools and supplies. She took the can of 3-in-l oil and went back to the house. While Dad was upstairs reading Clarence a story, she squirted oil in the end of several of Dad's cigars and put them back in the box.

The next morning as the Harts were leaving for church, Dad slipped a cigar into his pocket. After the service was over, he joined the other men outside and reached for his cigar. He struck a match to light it. When he put the match to the end of the cigar, there was a loud Poof! Flames leaped from the cigar!

Dad grabbed the cigar out of his mouth and threw it on the ground.

All the other men laughed so hard they could hardly talk. "Nick, you sure smoke high-powered cigars!" one of them finally sputtered.

Mr. Hart's face turned red, but he had nothing to say to the men. "It must be those kids," he muttered to himself.

That day at the dinner table, he asked, "Has anyone been fooling around with my cigars?"

Pierce and Hattie suddenly became very busy with their lunch. The rest of the children had blank expressions on their faces. They didn't know what Dad was talking about.

Later that evening, Dad was in the front room, sitting in his favorite chair. He started reading the newspaper, but the words began to blur. *Maybe if I light my pipe, I'll keep awake,* he thought. But after a few faintly soapy puffs, he still couldn't read the newspaper.

With his pipe dangling from his mouth, he leaned back in his chair, closed his eyes, and began to think over the minister's sermon of the morning. The *dominie* had encouraged the people to count their many blessings. Dad started to count his one by one—a wonderful family—a warm house—a good farm. Soon he fell asleep in the chair and his pipe dropped down beside him.

All of a sudden, Mom, who had been trying to get little Ervin asleep, smelled something burning, and it wasn't tobacco smoke she smelled! She ran out of the bedroom. There was Dad asleep in his chair. And the chair was smoking!

"Nick! Nick! Wake up!" screamed Mom. "Your chair is on fire!"

Just as Dad opened his eyes, the fabric of the chair burst into flames. He jumped up!

"Pierce! Hattie! Quick!" cried Dad. "My chair is on fire!"

Pierce and Hattie ran downstairs and helped Dad carry the chair out the front door. They threw it in the snow in the yard, but the chair continued to burn. It was ruined.

"I'm getting rid of my pipe and cigars right now!" Dad said. "They're too dangerous."

Hattie ran up the stairs and got on her knees by her bed. "Dear God, I prayed Dad would stop smoking, but I didn't mean for him to burn up! Thank you for teaching him a lesson and for keeping him safe!"

Chapter 3

Hattie's Hiding Place

*B*efore Hattie had opened her eyes, she knew that today would be a boring day—a long, boring day with nothing to do. She crawled out of bed and got dressed.

When she came downstairs for breakfast, the kitchen was a mess. Ervin was crying in his high chair. He had oatmeal on his face and in his hair. Clarence and Leona were fighting over a spoon with a fancy handle, and Pierce was trying to referee their fight.

Hattie didn't feel like eating breakfast in all that confusion. She quietly slipped out the door and headed for her secret hiding place in the maple grove.

No one but me, said Hattie, *will ever find my hiding place.* Hattie had to bend low under hanging branches to get to the trunk of her favorite tree. It was so tall that when she climbed to the top she thought she could see for miles.

Hattie had not been up in the tree very long when she heard Mom calling her name.

"Hattie! Hattie!" called Mom from the porch. "Telephone. It's Ruthie!"

Hattie hurried down the tree. Maybe this won't be a boring day after all.

"My mother says I can spend the day with you if it's okay with your mother," Ruthie said.

Hattie was excited at the thought. She turned to ask Mom.

"*Ya*, that would be nice," agreed Mom.

In a very short time, Mrs. Rhenn brought Ruthie to the Hart farm. "Have a good day. I'll be back for you around supper time," she said as Ruthie got out of the car.

Hattie grabbed two of her dolls and led Ruthie to her hiding place. "I'm the only one who knows about this," she told Ruthie. "This is my secret tree."

Hattie pulled herself up on a low branch. "Come on," she invited, holding her hand down to help Ruthie. "When you get high enough, you can see the whole countryside."

"I don't like to climb trees," Ruthie said. "Besides, I might tear my dress."

"You won't if you're careful, and this tree is easy to climb," Hattie replied.

Ruthie and Hattie had fun sharing secrets in the tree. They talked and talked and talked. It seemed only a little while had passed when Mom called, "Lunchtime, girls!"

Down the tree they scrambled. "Let's leave the dolls here. We'll come back right after lunch," Hattie suggested.

But later when they rushed back, someone else had been there. At the foot of the tree next to the dolls was a little box with Clarence's pet snake in it.

"Oh, no!" said Hattie. "Now we have to find another secret hiding place."

Hattie tucked her dolls under one arm, and grabbed Ruthie's hand with the other. Together they left the grove and ran out to the pasture.

"I know a place where they will never find us," said a determined Hattie.

The girls left the pasture and followed the fencerow. The weeds were high and prickly.

"Don't go so fast," said Ruthie. "I can't keep up with you. I've got things sticking to my skirt and the weeds are scratching my legs."

"We're almost there," said Hattie. "Keep going."

"Where are we going?" asked Ruthie in alarm.

"To an old sand pit. Pierce showed it to me. It's where they dug out sand to put on the dirt roads."

In a few minutes they were standing on the edge of the biggest hole in the ground Ruthie had ever seen.

"Here it is," said Hattie. She pointed down in the hole. "We can hide under that ledge, and no one will ever find us!"

"Jump!" said Hattie suddenly. And with one big leap, she was at the bottom of the pit.

"I'm scared," said Ruthie from up on the edge of the hole.

"Just close your eyes and jump," Hattie said. "I'll be here to catch you."

"First you want me to climb trees. Then you want me to jump down holes!" Ruthie protested. But she did as she was told.

"That wasn't too bad, was it?" asked Hattie.

"I guess not," said Ruthie. She brushed dirt from her dress.

"Isn't this a wonderful hiding place?" said Hattie as they crawled under the ledge.

"I'm tired and our dolls must be tired too," said Ruthie. "Let's rest for a few minutes."

The girls lay down, using their dolls for pillows. They had walked a long way and they were tired. Soon they were fast asleep.

When they woke up, it was getting dark.

"Oh, dear," said Hattie. "We must have slept for a long time."

"I'm supposed to be home for supper. My parents will be worried," Ruthie said with fear in her voice. "Let's crawl out of here and go back to your house."

They soon discovered that though it had been easy enough to jump into the pit, it wasn't that easy to get out. They tried to crawl up the steep sides of the pit, but the sand gave way under their feet. They kept slipping back to the bottom.

"What have you gotten us into?" wailed Ruthie. "What are we going to do?"

"Wait until someone comes and gets us," said Hattie.

"No one knows we're here," said Ruthie. "You said no one would find us if we hid in this pit. The sun has gone down and it's getting cold."

"We'll pray to God for help," said Hattie calmly. She was not easily discouraged. She reached out and held Ruthie's hands while she prayed.

"Dear God, no one knows where we are except You. Help others to find us, and help us to stay warm as long as they are looking. And don't let Mom and Mrs. Rhenn be too worried. Amen."

After they had prayed Ruthie felt better. "I guess all we can do is wait," she said.

Everything was very quiet, and it was getting darker and darker. Soon they heard a scratching sound and then a squeaking noise above their heads.

"Maybe it's a weasel coming to eat us," said Ruthie.

"Don't be silly," said Hattie. "Weasels don't eat people. It's probably a groundhog."

Next they heard a howling in the distance.

"I know those are wolves," Ruthie said tearfully.

"They do eat people!"

Hattie didn't know what to say to that. She just started praying again, only this time Hattie prayed God would give her an idea about how to get out of the pit. That's when it hit her. She grabbed the red cape that her doll was wearing.

"We could tie this red cloth to the end of a stick and wave it in the air," Hattie suggested.

"But it's too dark for anyone to see it," Ruthie said.

"Why don't we wrap it around a stone and throw it out of the pit?" Hattie asked. "Maybe someone will see it when they come looking for us."

For a long time, Hattie and Ruthie sat shivering in the dark. Finally they climbed back under the ledge to stay warm.

Carrying blankets and lanterns, Dad, Mr. Rhenn, and Pierce made their way to the sand pit. As the men came near the pit, Dad said, "Look, there's the cape from Hattie's doll. They must be close by."

They peered into the pit with the lanterns, but saw nothing.

"They aren't here," Dad said. Then he called, "Hattie! Hattie! Where are you? Please answer me!"

Hattie and Ruthie woke with a start. "Here we are! Here we are!" they cried as they crawled out from beneath the ledge.

Pierce jumped down into the pit. It took both Hattie and Pierce to help Ruthie up onto Pierce's shoulders.

"Here we are! Here we are!" they cried
as they crawled out from the ledge.

"I'm going to fall!" cried Ruthie, but Dad lay down at the edge of the pit while Mr. Rhenn held his legs. Dad reached down with his long arms and pulled Ruthie out.

Then Pierce bent over and Hattie scrambled onto his shoulders and grabbed Dad's hands. It was hardest to get Pierce out—he was heavier and had no one to boost him up. He ran up the sides of the pit a few times before he caught Dad's hands and pulled himself out.

When the dirty, weary girls returned to the house with the men, everyone laughed and cried at the same time. Their parents were so relieved that the girls were found, they forgot all about scolding them. Mom warmed some supper for the girls.

"I never knew I could be so hungry," Hattie told her mom.

"Yes," added Ruthie. "For a while, I thought we might be supper for the wolves!"

"Oh, I knew that was only an owl calling," said Hattie. "But I'm sure glad my secret place wasn't a secret from God!"

Chapter 4

The Writing Club

*O*ne day Hattie came home from school and went straight to the kitchen where Mom was making soup for supper. Hattie sat at the kitchen table and rested her chin in her hands.

I wish Ruthie wasn't mad at me, Hattie thought. *I miss being her best friend. Everywhere Ruthie goes, Lillian is there, too, like a shadow. I never have any time alone with Ruthie anymore.*

At last Mom noticed Hattie's troubled look. "Is there something wrong?" Mom asked.

"Yes," answered Hattie glumly. "I don't have any friends at school. At least, any friends I care about. Ruthie is mad at me because we had to stay in the pit at night."

"Ya, I thought it might be about Ruthie," said Mom. "I'm sure you two will get back together again soon, and it will be like old times."

"It will never be the same again!" declared Hattie

angrily. "Not with that dumb Lillian around all the time. She is Ruthie's best friend now."

"You can't change Ruthie and you can't pick her friends," said Mom. "Maybe you can find another friend you like just as well."

"Never! That will never happen!" Hattie said stoutly.

"Hattie, Hattie, your friends can't make you happy. That isn't what friends are for," Mom told her. But Hattie could see that Mom just didn't understand.

Lying in bed that night, Hattie kept thinking about her problem, turning it over and over in her mind. Then she had the perfect idea. She'd organize a club—a writing club! She'd call it The Writing Club of America.

Hattie and Ruthie both liked to write. And all the girls in her class could belong. She was certain that Miss Henry would be excited about her idea. Maybe the club could publish a newspaper once each month. That way Hattie and Ruthie would have to spend a lot of time together. Besides Lillian wasn't very interested in writing.

The next morning at school, Hattie shared her idea with Ruthie. "I'm starting a new club," she announced, "The Writing Club of America. You can be the first member."

"Do all the girls get to join?" asked Ruthie.

"Everyone who wants to," said Hattie, feeling very

generous. "We can meet today during lunchtime."

Word of Hattie's new club spread through the class during the morning. All the girls seemed interested in joining. Cloris, Mae, Dottie, Beatrice, Lola, Roberta, Ruthie, and Lillian. At lunchtime, Hattie took charge of the first meeting.

"Welcome to The Writing Club of America," said Hattie. "We are going to write a newspaper for the class each month. But first we have to elect officers. We need a president, and I think we should vote by secret ballot."

"I'd just as soon tell everyone who I want for president," declared Lola.

"That's not a good idea," said Hattie. "Some of us might be afraid to say out loud who we want to vote for. If we vote by secret ballot, we can vote for anybody in the class."

Hattie gave everyone a small piece of paper and a pencil. Of course, she hoped they would all vote for her. When everyone was finished, Lola collected the ballots, and Hattie read them out loud:

> *Cloris,*
> *Mae,*
> *Dottie,*
> *Beatrice,*
> *Lola,*
> *Roberta,*
> *Ruthie,*

Lillian,
and Hattie.

It took Hattie a minute before she realized what had happened. Everyone had voted for herself! Now what could they do?

Ruthie had a good suggestion. "We could vote for two people—for ourselves and for someone else."

"All right. That might work," Hattie agreed although she wasn't sure. She passed out more pieces of paper.

It took a little longer to figure out who to vote for this time. Hattie wrote down her name first and then she looked around. *I'll put down Lillian's name,* thought Hattie. *She'll feel bad if she doesn't get any votes and no one else will vote for her.*

Hattie collected the votes and read the names:

Cloris and Lillian,
Mae and Lillian,
Clara and Lillian,
Dottie and Lillian,
Beatrice and Lillian,
Lola and Lillian,
Hattie and Lillian,
Ruthie and Lillian,
Roberta and Lillian,
and Lillian and Ruthie

The last ballot that Hattie read was Lillian's. She had voted for Ruthie. Everyone else had voted for themselves and Lillian! Lillian had won!

Hattie didn't know what to say. Everyone else was speechless too. Each of them had voted for Lillian because they felt sorry for her, and thought she wouldn't get any votes.

Lillian broke the silence. "I decline to be president," she said quietly. "I wouldn't enjoy it and I wouldn't be any good at it."

"I like the idea of a club," said Cloris, "but I'm no writer. I'm backing out."

"Me too," said Mae. "We have plenty of writing to do in class without doing any more for a newspaper."

One by one, everybody withdrew from The Writing Club of America before the first meeting was over. Hattie was surprised, but she was glad. She didn't want a club that might be called the "Selfish Hattie Club."

Chapter 5

Ruthie on the Roof

*H*attie stared at the mirror in her bedroom, thinking. Lately she had been talking to her imaginary friend Evelyn Series in her mirror. Dad had warned her: "No more going out to the barn or under the apple tree or anywhere to talk to someone who isn't there. You're too old to be doing that, Hattie."

But Hattie couldn't get along without Evelyn Series yet. If she whispered quietly to her make-believe friend in the mirror, no one would discover her secret.

You look sad, said a voice from the mirror.

"I am," said Hattie. "That creepy Lillian has stolen my best friend, Ruthie."

I think I know how you feel, the voice said. *It's hard not to be jealous.*

"I'm not jealous," said Hattie. "Why should I be? Lillian is ugly and sniffs a lot."

"If that's all true, then why do you care?" asked

Evelyn Series.

"I'm mad," said Hattie. "She stole my best friend."

The door banged downstairs. "Where is everyone?" yelled Kathryn. "I'm home."

Hattie, jolted out of her reverie, ran down the stairs and hugged her older sister. Kathryn didn't come often, but it was good to see her when she did. "Kathryn! Kathryn! I didn't know you were coming to see us today," said Hattie.

Kathryn noticed Hattie's tangled hair and red eyes. "I'm glad I did. You look like you've lost your best friend," she said.

"I have," answered Hattie sadly.

Kathryn, always practical, said, "Find someone else to be your best friend. It worked for me. When Gertrude didn't want me around, Rena and I became good friends. Of course, that was before I married Lawrence and had a real best friend."

Hattie was sure Kathryn didn't have as much imagination and didn't care as much about having a good friend as Hattie did. But Kathryn's suggestion was the same one Mom had made. Maybe they were right. *At least*, Hattie thought, *I'll try it.*

The next day at school, Hattie went through the list of girls in her class. There was Clara who had no imagination, tattletale Charlotte, bossy Lola, and Mae and Cloris, who always stuck together. At least Beatrice was smart. *I guess she's the only possibility for my new best friend,* Hattie decided.

"Do you want to go talk and swing with me?" Hattie asked Beatrice at lunchtime.

"No, I get dizzy on the swings," said Beatrice.

"I suppose you don't like the teeter-totter, either," said Hattie.

"That's even worse," answered Beatrice.

Hattie decided that since Beatrice was such a bookworm, she would offer to let her read her favorite book, *Bad Little Hannah.*

"Oh, I read that two years ago," said Beatrice. "It was my Christmas present."

"Did your father give it to you?" asked Hattie, trying to make conversation.

"Oh, no, my father only gives me medical books. He wants me to become a doctor, but I don't want to be a doctor. I want to be a lawyer."

"I thought only men were doctors or lawyers," said Hattie.

Beatrice tossed her head. "You can be anything you want to be, if you're smart enough. My dad says I'm very smart," she said.

"Do you want to be a ball player? You could come to my house after school and play with my brothers and me," suggested Hattie.

"I need to study after school and I can't really waste my time playing," Beatrice said.

Hattie was discouraged, but she wasn't going to

give up. She was still determined to find a new best friend.

On the bus that evening, Arnold said to Hattie, "Why are you trying to be a friend to that boring Beatrice?"

"She's not boring. She's very smart," replied Hattie.

"Smart like a dictionary. All she ever does is throw big words around. She acts like she's read every book there is."

"Maybe she has," Hattie said.

The next day, Hattie decided to try to be friendly to someone else. She was sitting on the school steps at recess when she saw Cloris coming straight toward her, and Mae right behind.

Cloris and Mae were jealous of Ruthie because she was pretty and boys were always being silly around her. Cloris said that it was disgusting, and, of course, Mae agreed. They had also noticed that Ruthie was ignoring Hattie lately.

"Ruthie seems stuck up lately," Cloris said as soon as she had sat down beside Hattie. "She doesn't have time for anyone but that spooky Lillian."

Just hearing the very word *Lillian* made Hattie upset. "I know it," said Hattie. "She doesn't have time for me at all anymore."

"Maybe we should teach her a lesson," said Mae.
Hattie nodded.

"Here's my plan," said Cloris. "At lunchtime, let's ask Ruthie to eat lunch with us. We'll meet in back of the school."

"How will that teach her a lesson?" asked Hattie.

"Did you ever see that ladder leaning against the shed?" asked Cloris. "The one the janitor keeps against the building so he can get up on the roof to make repairs?"

"We'll think of an excuse to get Ruthie up the ladder and onto the roof," said Mae with a grin.

Hattie didn't understand what they were up to, but she was happy to be included, and didn't want to ask too many questions.

At lunchtime, Cloris said very sweetly to Ruthie, "How about eating lunch with us today? Hattie and Mae are coming too."

"Sure," answered Ruthie. "I usually eat with Lillian, but she's at home today."

After they had eaten their sandwiches, Cloris ran over to the shed and pretended to hear the chirp of a bird. "I think there's a little bird up there that's hurt," she called to the others.

"I hear it too," said Mae. "Somebody ought to go up there and see what's wrong with it."

"I'm not going to climb that ladder," said Hattie.

"Me, neither," said Cloris and Mae in unison.

"I guess I'll have to go," said Ruthie, and up the ladder she went.

As soon as Ruthie was on the roof, Mae and Cloris took the ladder and laid it on the ground.

Just then the bell rang, and Hattie, along with everyone else, rushed into the school. Their teacher had taught them never to be late. As Hattie threw herself quickly into her seat, she realized what she had done. *Oh no*, thought Hattie, *Poor Ruthie! How could I let them do that to her. She must feel terrible. I need to help her get down.*

Without another thought, Hattie jumped up and ran outside. There she found Ruthie huddled at the edge of the roof, sobbing quietly.

"Ruthie! Ruthie! I'll get the ladder. Don't worry, I'll get you down," cried Hattie.

Hattie picked up the heavy ladder and tugged it into place against the shed. Then she held it while Ruthie slowly came down. When Ruthie reached the ground, Hattie hugged her.

"Will you ever forgive me?" asked Hattie.

"Of course," said Ruthie. "You will always be my best friend!"

Hattie had waited for days and days to hear that.

"You will always be my best friend, too," said Hattie. She grabbed Ruthie's hand and they ran back into the school.

Chapter 6

Alone at the Festival

*E*very day at school Hattie could hear music coming from the gym. Once she had stopped and peeked in the door. There on the stage were girls from the eighth grade doing a Dutch folk dance. They wore matching costumes with sequins on the sleeves that sparkled as they twirled around. Hattie couldn't take her eyes off them. They were practicing for the Spring Festival.

But when the night of the festival came, no one in Hattie's family could take her. When she asked Dad if she could go to the Spring Festival, he said, "No, we're too busy. There will be plenty of chances for you to go when you get older."

"But I'm already ten years old and you never have time to take me anywhere." Hattie knew this wasn't true but she said it anyway.

"Why don't you go out and see what mischief Clarence and Leona have gotten into?" asked Mom.

Still thinking about how she could get to the festival, Hattie went outside. But she was not at all interested in what her little brother and sister were doing. She was still thinking about how she could go to the Spring Festival.

Why couldn't Mom and Dad take time for important things like this? Hattie complained. *Well, if everyone is too busy to take me, I'll just find a way to go myself.*

She sat down on the porch steps. *Maybe one of the neighbors will come by and take me,* thought Hattie. *I hope someone comes soon. I don't want to be late.*

Soon Hattie heard a car motor. If it was one of the neighbors, she would wave for them to stop. But it wasn't a neighbor. It was Mr. and Mrs. Norton. Mr Norton was the Fuller Brush man, who came by often to sell brushes of all kinds. He wanted to show Mom some combs and brushes. Mrs. Norton just came to visit.

"Looks like a young lady all dressed up with no place to go," laughed Mrs. Norton.

"That's right," said Hattie, looking very sorrowful. "I want to go to the Spring Festival, but my folks are too busy to take me."

The Nortons didn't know Hattie's mother and father had not given her permission. "Hop in," Mr. Norton said. "We'll take you and drop you off at the school." The Nortons thought the Harts would be grateful for their help. Hattie quickly jumped into the car, hoping no one would see her.

After I get to school, thought Hattie, *I'll tell Mr. Norton to let Mom and Dad know where I am. Dad will come and get me when the program is over.*

When they got to town, Mr. Norton drove straight to the school and let Hattie out. She hurried into the gym. Somehow she forgot all about asking Mr. Norton to let Dad know where she was.

The gym was full of people, but Hattie found an empty seat in the back. She spotted Beatrice and several students from her class, but Ruthie wasn't there. Hattie didn't care. She was excited when the curtain went up. For the next hour and a half, her eyes were glued to the stage. First, there was a short musical play about the Civil War. The singing was beautiful.

Then, a dark-eyed girl wearing a long white dress recited a poem. It was about a brave soldier who was stabbed in the back by a jealous rival just as he was coming home to his bride. It was so dramatic Hattie almost cried. Next, a boy recited a poem, but he was pretty nervous and Hattie felt sorry for him.

The band wasn't very big or very good, but Hattie was fascinated by the saxophone. She had always wanted to play the piano, but maybe a saxophone would be easier. The piano had so many keys.

In between poems and musical pieces, there were two "living paintings." The audience gasped as the curtain went up on the scene where students acted out Washington crossing the Delaware. The people on stage didn't move. They didn't even seem to be breathing.

The characters had elegant costumes, but Hattie thought they must be the students who couldn't sing or dance or speak very well. She hoped she would get a better part when she was old enough to be in the festival.

Finally, it was time for the dancers with the sequined sleeves. They were amazing! The dance was much better than it had looked when they practiced. How did so many girls do the same thing at the same time? No wonder they had started working right after the Christmas holidays. Hattie had never seen anything like it before.

Next year, I'll join the choir and the band and the drama club, thought Hattie. *Then I'll be ready when it's my turn to be in the eighth grade program.*

Hattie hardly noticed how much time had gone by until the program was over. Everyone was hurrying to pick up their children and take them home.

"Oh, I forgot to tell Mr. Norton to let Mom and Dad know where I am," said Hattie. "They'll wonder what happened to me!" Squeezing through the crowd, she ran down the stairs, hoping to get a ride with one of the neighbors. She saw the lights of cars in the parking lot, but she couldn't find anyone she knew. Finally everyone was gone, even the janitor.

There she was, all alone. "Now what do I do?" Hattie said out loud to herself. "Well, I've got two feet, and they're good for walking. I know the way home, and it's not very far."

She didn't realize it was three miles from the school to her home. Hattie started walking. *I'm glad there's a full moon, she thought.*

She walked and walked some more. She felt she'd walked forever. Then she saw a car coming. Mom had told her never to talk to strangers. She dived into the ditch at the side of the road. There she stayed, very quiet, not moving at all. After the car had passed, she got back on the road and continued walking.

"Keep walking, keep walking," she told herself. She started to count to pass the time away. "1, 2, 3, 4, 5, 6, 7. . . 1, 2, 3, 4, 5, 6, 7."

The gravel crunched beneath her feet. It was so quiet that every sound was loud. Even her breathing was noisy. She heard a screech owl in the distance and shivered. Then everything started looking and sounding scary.

Along the road the trees began to look like big monsters, with long arms reaching out to grab her. She picked up a stick. "Now I'll be able to protect myself," she said, trembling.

Off to the right, she saw a shape that looked like a

bear. It wasn't moving, but if she started to run, it might chase her, and it would be sure to catch her. She decided to scare it off instead. She ran toward the bear waving the stick and yelling, "Get out of here, get out of here," as loud as she could.

Whack! went the stick. But the bear didn't move. In fact, the bear wasn't a bear at all. It was only a big tree stump. Hattie felt better. *My imagination is running away with me,* she told herself. She kept on walking toward home.

Soon she was almost at the neighbor's house, where she'd leave the main road and walk down the dirt road to her house. It was then that she heard a dog howling at the moon. Hattie stood still. The dog, she knew, was a mean one that snarled at people. She wished he'd go under the porch to sleep so he wouldn't see her. But she couldn't stand in the road all night, waiting for the dog to stop howling. So she started walking again.

After she turned the corner, she realized she'd have to go past the graveyard to get home. Hattie was truly scared of graveyards. What if a ghost jumped out and attacked her?

"I will trust and not be afraid." said Hattie out loud. She tried to remember the Bible verses she had learned about not being afraid. One of her favorites came to mind: "Yea though I walk through the valley of the shadow of death, I will fear no evil for Thou art with me." If a graveyard wasn't the valley of the shadow of death, she didn't know what was!

She began to run as fast as she could repeating over and over, "I will trust and not be afraid. . . . I will trust and not be afraid. . . . I will trust and not be afraid."

Hattie never once looked at the gravestones. Her heart pounded in her ears and her stomach was doing flip-flops. She was out of breath and didn't think she could go one more step. A little voice inside Hattie kept saying, *Run, run, you're almost there!*

Hattie cried with relief when she finally reached the Harts' yard. She ran to the house and fell against the kitchen door, exhausted.

Dad heard the noise and opened the door. "Hattie! Where have you been?" he said. "We were worried sick about you!"

"Don't you know you're too young to be out after dark?" said Pierce.

The other children were crying and Mom had the telephone in her hand. She was calling the sheriff to tell him Hattie was lost. When she saw Hattie, she dropped the phone and ran and hugged her.

"Hattie, Hattie, mine *fanka*," she said. "We thought you were lost or maybe even dead. You've been gone for four hours. We've looked and called everywhere and no one knew where you were."

"I went to the school play," said Hattie, sniffing and catching her breath. "Mr. and Mrs. Norton came by and took me."

"How did you get home?" asked Clarence.

"I had to walk. I forgot to ask Mr. Norton to tell Mom and Dad to come for me."

"You walked?" said Pierce. "All three miles in the dark? Why, I could hardly do that!"

Pierce's words made Hattie feel very grown-up. Maybe she wouldn't tell them how scared she had been and about the dog and the graveyard. She'd just let them think she was really grown-up.

But she wouldn't go that far after dark by herself anymore. She knew that. And she would learn more Bible verses—just in case!

Chapter 7

The Scary Straw Stack

*S*pring was coming, and the youngest Hart children wanted to play outdoors with Hattie.

"Hattie, Hattie, play wif me," said little Ervin.

"Let's play hide-and-seek today?" begged Leona.

"Come on, Hattie, let's all go, um . . . have some fun," Clarence finished brightly.

"I've got an idea for some real fun," said Pierce. "Let's slide down the barn roof!"

"Mom and Dad won't like it," said Leona.

"Mom and Dad aren't here," said Hattie. "And it sounds like fun to me."

"It's too high," said Clarence, looking up.

Pierce ran to get a ladder and Hattie helped him put it up against the barn. The roof had a tar paper covering. It was hard to climb up to the peak because the roof was slippery, but it was wonderful for sliding down. It was as much fun as the Ferris wheel at the fair.

But on Hattie's first try she slid off the edge of the roof and landed on a pile of lumber.

"Ouch! Ouch! Ouch!" she cried. "That hurt!"

Hattie sat down rubbing her leg. Then she noticed the tall stack of straw that Dad and the men had made with the threshing machine last fall.

"Let's slide down the straw stack," suggested Hattie.

"No," said Pierce, "that's not a good idea. Dad doesn't want straw spread all over the yard. That straw is for the cows to eat until a new crop of hay is ready."

"I'm not going to ruin the straw stack," said Hattie. "I'm just going to slide down once."

"We're going to be in enough trouble with Dad for sliding down the roof of the barn," said Pierce. "I don't want any part of your foolishness. Anyway, it's time for Clarence and me to do our chores before Dad gets back home at noon."

Pierce and Clarence left for the barn. Hattie and Leona walked over to the straw stack. Little Ervin toddled behind them. They stood looking at the stack for a moment, and it didn't look so high to Hattie.

"I'm going to climb to the top and slide down just once," Hattie said. "You can watch. Leona, you and Ervin stand back and wait for me."

Hattie began climbing, the straw slipping beneath her feet. It was hard work and she had to stop to catch her breath, but at last she got to the top.

"I'm an eagle, perched on top of the highest mountain in the world," Hattie announced to her brother and sister gazing up at her. She jumped up and down on the springy straw, wildly waving her arms. Bounce, bounce, bounce went her feet.

Then she started sliding down the slippery straw. It was such fun, she did it again! Every time she climbed back up, the straw pile seemed to get shorter and wider.

"This is so much fun," Hattie called out.

Soon the straw stack was only half as high as when she had started, and straw was spread all over the yard.

"I better quit," said Hattie as she slid down the stack for the last time. "Come on," she called to Leona and Ervin. "Let's go back to the house now."

When Dad came home at noon, he saw right away that the straw stack was ruined. One look at Hattie was enough to tell him that she had been on the straw stack. Straw was still sticking in her hair.

"Hattie, I didn't warn you before," said Dad, "but we need to keep the straw in a round stack so the water will run off when it rains. If the straw gets wet, we can't use it in the barn. Promise me you won't slide down again."

"I promise," said Hattie. She was truly sorry for what she had done.

The next day, Hattie, Leona, and Ervin went to see how Dad had restacked the straw.

"It looks like it did before," Hattie said. She walked around the pile, looking it up and down.

"Don't you dare slide down it!" warned Leona. "Dad said not to!"

"I'm not going to," Hattie said. "I'm just going to touch the straw to see if it still feels and smells the same as it did yesterday."

"If you don't get near it, you won't climb it," Leona said. "I think I'm going to call Mom."

Hattie could hardly resist climbing, but she had promised Dad and she meant to keep her word.

Just then, little Ervin, started toddling toward Hattie.

"Want Hattie to make you a tunnel to hide in?" asked Hattie.

"Tunnel to hide!" he said eagerly.

"Dad said to leave the straw alone," warned Leona again. Leona was always ready to act as Hattie's conscience.

"Dad said not to slide on it," Hattie said. "He didn't say we couldn't build a tunnel."

Leona couldn't think of anything to say to this, and soon they were busy digging on one side of the straw stack. They were using their hands as shovels to pull the straw out.

"Come here, Ervin," directed Hattie. "Your secret

hiding place is ready for you."

Ervin happily crawled into the waiting hole. "Hide in my tunnel," he chirped.

Hattie, never happy with a job half done, called out to Leona, "Let's go dig on the other side. Maybe we can make a tunnel all the way through."

Leona thought this was a good idea, so they went to the other side and began digging. Several minutes later, Hattie went to check on Ervin in his hiding place. She hurried to the other side of the stack.

But Ervin wasn't anywhere in sight! The straw had slid down from the top. It had covered the hole where the tunnel was, and little Ervin wasn't anywhere in sight.

"Quick, Leona!" Hattie yelled. "We've got to get Ervin out of here before he dies because he doesn't have any air!"

Hattie and Leona began digging wildly. Straw flew through the air as Hattie shouted, "We're coming, Ervin. We're coming!"

Then Hattie began to be afraid that she couldn't get to Ervin in time to save him. She rushed to the house, yelling at the top of her voice: "Mom! Mom! Come quick! Ervin has suffocated!"

Hattie dashed into the kitchen. "Oh, Mom, I think Ervin is dead," Hattie cried.

"Ervin not dead," called her little brother, who came running from the dining room.

"Come here, Ervin," said Hattie.
"Your secret hiding place is ready for you."

Hattie nearly fainted. She grabbed Ervin and kissed him again and again.

"I have to get out of tunnel. I have to go see Mama," explained Ervin as well as he could.

"Oh, Ervin, you're alive," burst out Leona. She had followed Hattie into the house.

Mom wasn't sure what had happened. "How about some nice cool lemonade?" She wisely suggested, trying to calm the girls.

"My throat is dry," Hattie said, sinking into a chair.

"This will help," said Mom, handing her a glass of lemonade.

"Will it help my thumping heart and jiggly stomach?" Hattie wondered.

"Maybe we could add a few cookies for that," Mom suggested. "Now could you tell me what happened?"

"I learned a good lesson," Hattie said. "When Dad tells me not to slide on the straw stack, I will leave it alone. I don't want to lose Ervin ever again!

Chapter 8

Tricks

*H*attie was in the front yard in a sea of dandelions. She and Pierce were trying to entertain Clarence, Leona, and Ervin. Puzzle, the cat, ran through the children's legs, pawing at the white puffs.

In her hands Hattie held a huge dandelion with a white fluffy head. It was just right for blowing. Closing her eyes, Hattie said softly:

> *Starlight, star bright,*
> *First star I see tonight.*
> *I wish I may, I wish I might*
> *Have the wish I wish tonight.*

It didn't matter to Hattie that it wasn't nighttime or that the dandelion wasn't a star. She puckered her lips, ready to blow.

Suddenly a big breath of air whizzed past her, and all she held in her hands was a bare dandelion stem. She was furious.

"Pierce, you meany!" shouted Hattie. She ran after

him, grabbing the back of his shirt. Pop went the buttons on his front.

"Now look what you've done, Spitfire Hitchie," Pierce yelled. "You've ripped the buttons right off my shirt."

Hattie didn't like being called "Spitfire Hitchie." She yelled back at Pierce, "I didn't yank the buttons off your shirt. I held your shirt and you pulled away. You tore those buttons off your own shirt!"

"Stop it!" said Mom, coming out of the house. "Stop your fighting. Pierce, you had better come in if you can't stop teasing Hattie. You need to work on your book report for class tomorrow. Hattie can take care of the children without your help."

"I'll get even with you!" Pierce muttered to Hattie as he went inside. Book reports were his least favorite things to do.

He didn't wait very long to get back at Hattie. When Hattie crawled in bed that night, something cold and slimy touched her toes.

"Help! Help!" screamed Hattie so loud that Dad heard her from the parlor. The whole family came running up the stairs to see what was wrong.

"Something terrible is in my bed!" screamed Hattie. "It almost bit me!"

Dad threw back the covers and out jumped a little frog. "Who did this?" asked Dad sternly.

"I did," admitted Pierce, knowing that Dad would

find out sooner or later.

"Why did you do it?" asked Dad.

"I couldn't find a snake, so I had to use a frog," said Pierce, pleased with his joke.

"I don't think that's funny," said Dad. "You scared Hattie and the rest of us too. We thought something terrible had happened."

Dad hardly ever spanked Pierce, so Hattie was surprised when he said, "Young man, to the woodshed!"

Hattie listened carefully but she didn't hear a thing from the woodshed. If Dad really did spank Pierce, he didn't spank him very hard. The next day, Pierce acted as though nothing had happened.

"Want to play follow the leader?" he asked that afternoon after he had finished doing his chores.

"Yes," said Hattie.

"Okay, I'm the leader and you follow me," said Pierce importantly.

"That sounds easy," said Hattie. She didn't know if she could keep up with Pierce, but she would soon find out. He had long legs and he ran very fast. Into the grove of trees and back again ran Pierce. Then he headed toward the barn and disappeared inside.

Hattie ran after him, determined to keep up. Coming into the barn from the bright sunlight, it was very dark. Hattie could hardly see anything. Just in time, she saw Pierce go through an open window in the back of the barn.

I can do anything Pierce can do, Hattie thought. She climbed on the low windowsill, just as Pierce had done, and jumped to the ground below.

"Oh, no! What is this?" cried Hattie. She had landed right in the middle of a manure pile.

"You didn't jump far enough," laughed Pierce.

Hattie didn't laugh. She tried to keep back her tears as she ran to the house to wash the manure off her shoes.

"Phew! What happened to you?" asked Clarence holding his nose.

After Hattie explained, Mom shook her head, "Ya, that was a bad thing for Pierce to do. Dad may have to take him to the woodshed again."

"No, I'm going to think of a trick to play on him," Hattie said with determination.

The days were getting longer as Spring came, and Pierce and Dad worked outside later each day. On Saturday night after supper, Pierce said, "I'm tired. I've worked hard today. I'm going to lie down on the grass under the apple tree."

The rest of the Hart children were in the yard, playing games. Mom was sitting on the porch, crocheting.

"I know a better way to rest than lying down," said Hattie. "I read about it in a book Miss Henry loaned me."

*She started moving back, one step at a time,
across the yard and away from Pierce.*

Pierce was interested. "From a book, huh?"

"Here, I'll show you," Hattie said. "Stand right here. Put your hands together in front of you. I'll stand in front of you and put my hands out about eight inches apart. See if you can move your hands up and down between my hands without touching them. It's kind of like hypnotism."

"That's easy," said Pierce.

"Yes, but you have to do it blindfolded. That way you can really relax," said Hattie. She folded a handkerchief and tied it around Pierce's head.

"I won't have any trouble," Pierce replied.

"Now, count to fifty when I say start," said Hattie. "No one has been able to do this more than fifty times. You have to count out loud and not too fast."

Pierce started counting. "One, two, three, four—"

"You're good," said Hattie.

"Five, six, seven, eight, nine, ten—"

"Not so fast," said Hattie.

"Eleven . . . twelve . . . thirteen," Pierce counted slower.

"That's right. You'll be feeling relaxed soon," Hattie encouraged him. She started moving back, one step at a time, across the yard and away from Pierce.

Pierce kept right on moving his hands up and down and counting.

Dad came out on the porch. He saw Pierce standing there wearing a blindfold and wondered what he was doing. He looked ridiculous. Then Dad saw Mom and Clarence doing their best to keep from bursting out laughing. Hattie was doubled over with silent laughter.

"What's going on here?" asked Dad. "Are you trying to do some magic trick, Pierce? If so, you have a big audience."

Pierce tore the blindfold off his eyes while the rest of the family collapsed in laughter. Pierce knew he had been fooled, but he grinned.

"All right, Hattie. No more 'Spitfire Hitchie'," he said. "I guess the one who laughs last laughs best."

Chapter 9

The Haunted House

*H*attie and her best friend Ruthie Rhenn were walking by an old house on the outskirts of town. They kept carefully to the far side of the street. They didn't want to get too close to the house just in case what they had heard about it happened to be true.

The girls' eyes took in the peeling paint and rickety stairs. Weeds were growing over the path leading to the door. Everyone said that an old man lived there, but the girls had never seen him.

"It sure looks spooky to me," said Hattie.

"I wonder why he keeps the shades pulled down?" Ruthie asked, in a whisper.

"I suppose so people can't peek in," Hattie guessed. "Arnold told me that a man in a uniform brings food to the house. Lillian lives right next door, and she says he brings it late at night."

"Do you suppose the man who lives there is a

criminal and he's hiding from the law?" asked Ruthie. She was looking at the ramshackle house with the shutters closed tight.

"He must have done something wrong," agreed Hattie. "Why else would he want to hide from everyone?"

Hattie could tell that the house had once been beautiful. It had a big oak door and gray siding. If only the owner cared enough to paint the house and mow the yard, it could be pretty again. Too bad its new owner was a criminal!

The girls continued on their way to Ruthie's house. Later that night Hattie asked her father about the haunted house.

"You must be talking about the old Wiersma house," Dad said, rubbing his chin. "I don't know who lives there now. The Wiersmas built the house, and they were very wealthy. That house used to be the pride of our town. But the Wiersmas had some hard times and had to move. The house has been empty for a long time now. I'm glad someone moved into it."

Hattie just wanted to know that the new owner wasn't someone who would do the neighbors harm.

A week later, Lillian came to school one morning very excited. She had some news she couldn't wait to share with Ruthie and Hattie.

"Guess what I saw last night when I came home

from school?" she whispered.

"What?" asked Hattie and Ruthie together.

"Well . . . " said Lillian slowly, who liked being the center of attention, "last night a car pulled up and stopped in front of that mysterious house next door to mine. That same man who brings the groceries, brought a girl about our age. They got out of the car and walked into the house."

"Oh! Tell us—what else did you see?" asked Hattie.

"Something very strange," Lillian said, her eyes shining with excitement. "The man who came in the car left, but the little girl wasn't with him. He left her in the house with that criminal!"

The three girls looked at each other in horror. What would happen to the poor little girl who had been left in the haunted house!

Lillian agreed to keep an eye on the house for any more signs of the little girl. But several days had passed and Lillian had not seen her again. Hattie decided to tell Mom what had happened.

"Hattie," said Mom patiently, "sometimes things aren't what they look like. You don't know everything, so you should not be getting ideas. Ya, Hattie, you have such an imagination! Sometimes you see things and hear things, but they didn't really happen. Before you spread any rumors, learn the truth."

Hattie knew Mom was right, but before she was

tempted to ignore Mom's words, she discovered who the little girl was. The next day she walked into Hattie's classroom.

"We have a new student joining our class," said Hattie's teacher, Miss Henry. "This is Mary Ann Webster from New York. She has just moved to town."

Miss Henry seated Mary Ann at an empty desk at the back of the room next to Hattie. Then, the teacher suggested that Hattie introduce Mary Ann to her friends at recess. Hattie nodded. She couldn't take her eyes off this mysterious new classmate with her brown curls and blue eyes and fancy store-bought dress.

As the class was going out to the playground at recess, Hattie's classmate Arnold came up behind her. "Be careful, Hattie," he said. "She lives in the house with a ghost! She might cast a spell on you!"

"Can't scare me," Hattie hissed, giving Arnold a dirty look. But what he said did give her goose bumps.

During recess, Mary Ann stayed close to Hattie. She seemed shy and nervous. Hattie tried to introduce Mary Ann to her friends, but the rest of the girls avoided her.

Hattie pretended not to notice. She decided she would be nice to Mary Ann, even though no one else was. *Isn't that what God would want me to do?* she asked herself. And anyway, Hattie liked Mary Ann.

In spite of being quiet and shy, she told interesting stories about New York City. Hattie liked hearing about faraway places she had only imagined.

But there might be a price to pay for this mysterious new friend. Hattie was afraid of what her other friends might think if she spent too much time being kind to Mary Ann. And worst of all—what if Arnold was right?

"I tell you, Hattie, she will cast a spell on you, and her ghost will follow you wherever you go!" Arnold shouted at Hattie on the school bus as they were riding home.

Arnold leaned close and whispered over the seat. "Me and some of the other boys are going to scout out that haunted house tomorrow. We're going to knock on the door and ask to talk to the old man," he bragged. "After we've met him, we're going to tell a policeman all about him. Citizens are supposed to tell about criminals who are hiding from the law, you know. When they find out, it's their duty."

Hattie smiled. She thought Arnold and his friends would be too scared to ever get to the door of the house. Actually, they almost made it, but when they saw a light go on inside, they ran away as fast as they could.

Hattie wished Arnold would hush. She was glad the next day was a holiday and there would be no school.

On Monday, at lunchtime, Cloris and Mae came up to Hattie. "Did you turn into a ghost yet?" Cloris asked.

That was too much for Hattie! "Ghosts are make-believe," she said to the two girls. "Anybody with any sense at all knows that!"

She turned on her heel and stalked off. She was going to ask Mary Ann right then and there just what was going on in that house. She found Mary Ann sitting alone on a bench, nibbling on a sandwich. Hattie sat down beside her.

"Who's that old man who lives in your house?" Hattie blurted out.

Startled, Mary Ann looked at Hattie. Then she looked away. "My grandfather," she answered.

"Your grandfather?" Hattie repeated. She couldn't believe it! "Where's the rest of your family?" she asked.

"I don't have any other family," Mary Ann said sadly, putting the rest of her sandwich back into her lunch pail. "My mother and father were killed in a train wreck last year. Grandfather is all the family I have."

Hattie, used to being surrounded by brothers and sisters, aunts and uncles, found it hard to believe that Mary Ann only had a grandfather. Hattie felt so sad for her. She wanted to punch Arnold for spreading all those rumors about Mary Ann.

When they saw a light go on inside,
they ran away as fast as they could.

"Do you like living with your grandfather?" Hattie asked. How could anyone like living in such a creepy house?

But Mary Ann surprised her. The girl's blue eyes lit up and she smiled. "Oh, yes! He's very kind," she said.

This didn't sound like the old man Hattie had imagined hiding in the haunted house. "But why doesn't he ever come out?" she asked.

Mary Ann bit her lip and looked down at the lunch pail on her lap.

But Hattie asked another question before she could answer. "What does he do for a living?" she prodded.

This time Mary Ann replied. "He's a doctor," she whispered. "But please, please! Don't tell anyone I told you that. He doesn't want anyone to know!"

"Well, why not?" Hattie asked, her eyes wide. "Being a doctor is a good thing. Why would anybody want to hide it when he's a doctor and could be out helping people?"

Mary Ann started crying. "I can't tell you why."

Hattie felt terrible. She had made Mary Ann cry. *Poor Mary Ann.* She seemed so alone. The other kids at school were making up all kinds of lies about her. Hattie put her arms around her friend. "I'm sorry, Mary Ann," she said.

Hattie felt even more guilty when Mary Ann didn't come to school the next day. A whole week went by, and still Mary Ann did not come to class. Hattie was afraid that she and the other boys and girls had driven her away.

When the second week went by, Hattie began to be afraid that Mary Ann's grandfather was keeping her from coming to school. Maybe he even had the poor girl locked up in chains in the basement of that old house!

I'm going to rescue Mary Ann! Hattie decided. *That's what friends are for.*

Chapter 10

Mary Ann's Mystery

*H*attie was very worried about Mary Ann, especially after she'd been absent from school for two weeks.

On Friday night at supper, Hattie said bravely, "I just know something bad is going on in that old house. I'm going over to Mary Ann's and find out what is wrong."

Dad looked at her as he said, "It's time for our Bible reading." Then he opened the Bible and began to read verses from the sixth chapter of Proverbs:

> *These six things does the Lord hate; yea, seven are an abomination unto him: A proud look, a lying tongue, and hands that shed innocent blood, a heart that deviseth wicked imaginations, feet that be swift in running to mischief, a false witness that speaketh lies, and he that soweth discord among the brethen.*

Closing the Bible, Dad looked at Hattie again. "Gossip is a very bad thing," he said. "It usually is far from the truth and it does people a lot of harm."

"But, Dad," said Hattie, "what if something looks like the truth, and if you tell others about it, you could do something to help?"

"Are you sure, Hattie, that it is the truth, or is it just your imagination?" Dad asked with a serious look on his face. "You would not want to hurt someone by spreading false stories."

"Listen, Hattie," said Pierce, leaning forward in his chair, "Mr. Van Gelder told us at our Young Peoples' Society meeting that telling lies about someone is as bad as hitting that person with an axe or a sword."

Hattie frowned at her older brother.

"It's true!" he said. "We looked it up in Proverbs for ourselves."

Hattie was sure that Pierce didn't know what he was talking about. But Dad's words had put a little doubt in her mind. What if all those things she had told Ruthie were not true? She should have stopped the class from gossiping about Mary Ann and her grandfather and she should have quit gossiping herself!

"Well, I'm going over to that house and find out what's wrong," said Hattie bravely.

"That's a good idea," said Mom. "I think Mary Ann could use a friend, and you can be of help to her."

Saturday morning came. Hattie walked up to Mary Ann's house, praying with every step she took.

She knocked on the door, but there was no answer. She knocked again, hoping no one was home. She was about to run away when the door opened.

"May I help you?" asked a kind old gentleman. It was Mary Ann's grandfather.

"Is. . . is. . . Mary Ann sick?" stammered Hattie.

"I was sick, but I'm okay now," Mary Ann said cheerfully from inside. "Hattie is my best friend, Grandfather. May she come in?"

"Yes, yes, do come in," he said in the same kind voice.

Before Hattie had a chance to sit down, Mary Ann said, "Would you like to have some cookies that I baked?"

"Yes, please," said Hattie, trying to get her voice back. Hattie looked around. Everything was neat and clean. She noticed a beautiful lamp on the table and a hand-carved rocker in one corner. They looked very fancy to Hattie.

"Oh, Hattie, I'm so glad you came. This is a happy day for us, and I wanted to tell you first." Mary Ann looked at her grandfather and he smiled and nodded. "Grandfather's name has been cleared."

Hattie didn't know what in the world she was talking about, but it sounded like a mystery was going to be solved.

Mary Ann's grandfather began to explain. "Back in New York, a promising young doctor and I worked together in a hospital there. He was still in training. We performed an operation together on a wealthy patient and it should have been a simple operation. But my young doctor friend gave him the wrong medicine and the patient died. The nurse had given us the wrong chart.

"I had to make a choice. I had already decided to retire, and I hated to see a brilliant young doctor lose his license because of an honest mistake. So I decided to take the blame and go into hiding. That way, I wouldn't have to explain anything, and my doctor friend could continue to practice medicine."

"But Grandfather, tell her the happy news," Mary Ann said.

"Oh, yes," said Grandfather, beaming. "The man who drove my car for me was the only one who knew I was hiding in this old house that belonged to my father. He came yesterday with the news that my doctor friend had been cleared for his part in the error. Now he wants me to come back to New York and work with him again."

"Oh, Hattie, isn't that wonderful news?" Mary Ann was smiling as broadly as her grandfather.

"Will you have to go back to New York when your grandfather goes?" asked Hattie. She didn't want

Mary Ann to go.

"Yes, but I hate to leave. You have become my very best friend. But I only came here to be with Grandfather. Back in New York, I have a governess who stays with me. I love her, but I love my grandfather best of all." Mary Ann gave him a big hug.

Hattie could hardly believe what she had just heard. "I'm glad the mystery is solved, but I'm sorry I thought your grandfather was a criminal living in a haunted house."

"I knew something was wrong," said Mary Ann. "But you always stayed my friend and I'm glad you did. Now would you like a cookie?"

Hattie would miss Mary Ann. She was glad she had been Mary Ann's friend, but she was sorry she had said bad things about her grandfather. Now she knew Dad was right, and so was the Bible, when they talked about being a false witness.

Just wait until I tell the real story of the Haunted House! she thought.

Chapter 11

Dancing with the Mayor

*H*attie couldn't remember wanting anything as much as she wanted to visit her cousins in Orange City. Besides it was time for the Tulip Festival.

"I could take the train," Hattie begged her dad. "I'm old enough to go alone."

"Maybe you're old enough, but do you know how much money that would cost?" exclaimed Pierce. "We don't have that kind of money."

"I guess you're right," Hattie said with a sigh. She knew taking a fifty-mile trip on the train would cost a lot of money.

"Maybe we could all go," said Dad. "It wouldn't cost too much to drive to Orange City. And I have a few days to spare. It's too wet to work in the fields."

"You mean we could all go?" asked Hattie, her eyes wide.

"Every one of us?" chimed in Clarence.

"Yes, all but Pierce. He's been to the festival before, and he needs to stay home and take care of things here on the farm."

"We can stay overnight at Aunt Rica's," said Dad.

"Overnight? All of us? At Aunt Rica's? Oh, Dad! You're wonderful!" said Hattie.

The next day they were packed and ready to leave.

"It's going to be a squishy ride," said Leona, who did not like to ride in a crowded car.

"Better not complain," said Hattie, "or we might have to stay home after all."

"Pile in and let's go," said Dad.

"I get the window. I'm oldest since Pierce isn't coming," said Hattie.

"I'm next oldest," announced Clarence.

"It's not fair. I always have to sit in the middle. We should take turns," said Leona.

"That's enough," Dad said with a stern look.

Leona stayed in the middle, frowning. Little Ervin climbed on to Hattie's lap so they could share the window. Clarence sat on the other side, and Mom sat up front with Dad.

"See, everybody has a window but me. It's not fair," said Leona.

"When we are halfway there, you can trade with Clarence," said Dad.

"Roll the window down. I need some air. I can

hardly breathe!" Leona said next.

"No, it will ruin my hair. It's blowing all over," said Hattie.

Finally Dad said in exasperation, "I can stop the car, you know, and make you walk."

"We're almost there," encouraged Mom. "Ya, I think we turn pretty soon."

At last Hattie recognized Uncle Sip's chicken house. "We're here!" she cried.

Aunt Rica, Uncle Sip, and their seven children greeted them. Aunt Rica kissed Mom who was her sister, and then she kissed all the children!

Supper was on the table, and everyone scurried in and tried to find an empty space to sit down. Some had to wait and take turns, but no one seemed to mind. Aunt Rica was good at making everyone feel at home.

Finding a place to sleep was something else. The boys had a bedroom and the girls had a bedroom. They slept across the beds so everyone would have a place to lie down.

Hattie had to bend her knees so her feet wouldn't hang off the bed, but she didn't want to complain to Aunt Rica.

In the guest room, where Mom and Dad slept, Aunt Rica pulled out the bottom drawer of the big dresser. She laid the drawer on the floor and padded it with blankets so little Ervin would have a place to sleep.

The next morning everyone was in a scramble trying to get dressed and have breakfast."Maybe pancakes wasn't the best thing to cook," admitted Aunt Rica. Mom had to wipe sticky syrup off the clean shirts of both Clarence and Ervin.

"They're as good as new," said Mom. "I think you boys were too excited to remember to be careful."

Dad and Uncle Sip came in from the parlor where they had been drinking their coffee. "It's Tulip Festival time. Is everybody ready to go?" asked Uncle Sip.

"It isn't very far into town," said Aunt Rica. "We were planning to walk. We have plenty of time so we won't miss any of the parade."

Hattie wondered if people thought they were all one big family. Why, someone might even think all fourteen kids were brothers and sisters! She decided to walk several feet behind the others so she wouldn't look like part of the group.

"Listen," said Clarence after they were in town. "I hear band music. Maybe the parade has started." He started running and the rest of the kids tried to keep up with him.

Hattie was fascinated. A sea of tulip blooms was everywhere she looked—beds of orange blooms surrounded by yellows and reds, waves of pink against white. Many of the tulips had been planted in designs. There were stars and windmills and barns and crosses and rings and both the American and the Dutch flags—all made with tulips.

"There must be millions of tulips," Hattie said to her mother.

"Ya, it looks like Holland for sure," said Mom. She was smiling a big smile.

I want to be right up front, thought Hattie, *where all the action is.* And she plunked herself down on the curb in front of everyone.

"Here come the street sweepers," one of her cousins yelled.

"Street sweepers always lead the parade," Dad had told Hattie. It was a tradition from the old country, where Dad and many of the people from Orange City used to live. Each morning the citizens of the town went through the cobblestone streets splashing water on the street and sweeping them clean with big push brooms.

"But the streets here aren't too dirty," said Hattie.

"We do it to remind us of what it was like in Holland," Dad replied.

The sweepers' feet clunked as they walked in their wooden shoes and swished their brooms. The women twirled around in their starched, full skirts and white peaked bonnets.

Hattie was so busy watching them, she almost missed the mayor's entrance. When she heard loud music, she jumped up to see better. First she saw a little boy carrying a sign that said, "The Burgermiester of Orange City." Then she saw the mayor coming down the street, surrounded by pretty girls in Dutch dresses and wooden shoes.

All of a sudden the little boy who was carrying the sign tripped and fell. His sign flew through the air and landed right at Hattie's feet.

Hattie jumped off the curb. She helped the little boy to his feet and handed him the sign.

The *burgermeister* stopped in front of Hattie. "Thank you for your quick thinking, little miss," he said. He took her hand. "I'd like you to come and dance with me."

Never in a hundred years would Hattie have dreamed this would happen! She was dancing with the mayor in the Tulip Festival parade! They danced down the street all the way to the end of the parade.

Hattie was dazed as she returned to her spot on the curb by her family!

But the highlight of the parade was still to come— the appearance of the Tulip Festival queen. Hattie was starstruck when she saw her coming. *Someday I want to be the queen and wear a crown of jewels and a dress of shimmering pink satin and carry a wand that glitters in the sunshine,* thought Hattie.

Next came the floats. Comments drifted out of the crowd behind Hattie as each new float came by.

"Look at that windmill made out of flowers?"

"Everything is made of flowers on that one, even the girl's skirt," said Aunt Rica.

The girl on that float isn't any older than I am, thought Hattie. *Look at her beautiful costume.*

"Those horses, they're huge—but I guess they have to be to pull that wagon."

"There's a boat made out of flowers."

"Oh, look at the beautiful silver harnesses on the horses pulling that one."

After more bands, more Dutch dancers, more floats, finally the parade was over, at least for that year.

As the family walked back to Aunt Rica's house, everyone was talking at once.

"Boy, were you lucky to be down in front!" said Clarence. "But weren't you scared when the burgermiester asked you to dance?"

"Not a bit," said Hattie. "It was thrilling. I wish the Tulip Festival would last forever!"

Chapter 12

Easter Joy

"I can't wait to color eggs," said Hattie as she filled four cups with water. Then she put four small bottles of food coloring—red, green, orange, and blue—on the table. Hattie had colored eggs for Easter every year since she could remember.

The small children watched as Hattie dropped food coloring into each cup of water and changed it to a cup of magical color.

Mom came into the kitchen with a basket of hardboiled eggs. She gave each child a teaspoon to fish the eggs out of the water after they were colored. She explained how it was done as she spread newspapers on the table to catch the splashes.

Leona knew just which color she would use. She wanted her egg to look like the pretty blue robin eggs she had seen in nests around the Hart farm.

Hattie took a crayon and drew a cross on one of the eggs. After she dipped the egg in the colored water, the cross was still there. "I'm making this egg to take to Lillian's little brother. He is crippled and never gets to church so at least he ought to hear something about Jesus at Easter. I think I could tell him a story about Jesus, couldn't I, Mom?"

"Ya, it's worth trying," Mom agreed.

Clarence drew some fish on his egg. He wanted to dye the egg blue so the fish would be swimming in water. But Leona's egg wasn't done yet, so he used green.

After the eggs were all colored, Hattie set them carefully back in the basket and left it on the table.

The next morning, she popped out of bed, eager to find her Easter surprise. Mom always hid small Easter gifts in the yard and everyone dashed outside on Easter morning to find their treasures.

Then it was time to get ready for church. "I can't wait for everyone to see my beautiful dress," Leona said. She twirled around to make her skirt swing out.

Hattie felt just as beautiful, but she was old enough not to say it. Dad had sold the hogs for good prices this spring, so both girls had new Easter dresses.

"Hurry," said Dad, "or we will be late for church." Hattie was always the last one in the car. She needed extra time to comb her curly hair. She had finally learned to use the curling iron without burning her fingers or her hair.

When the Harts got to church, they filed into their usual pew. Mom looked down the row of children in their Easter clothes and happy faces. She couldn't help but be proud of her family.

At first Hattie sat very quietly thinking how elegant she must look in her dress. But then she started listening. As the dominie read the story of Jesus' death on the cross, Hattie thought, *Why would they do that? Jesus never did a wrong thing in his whole life.*

Almost as though he had heard Hattie's question, the pastor said, "Jesus died on that cross because He loved us. The good news is that Jesus is alive and lives in heaven today—and He still loves us."

At the close of the service, everyone sang "Up from the Grave He Arose." Hattie sang loudest of all.

When Hattie got home and took off her new dress, she started thinking. *Leona and I had something new to wear but Mom didn't. All she had to wear for Easter was her same old white blouse and black skirt.*

I wonder, thought Hattie, *if there's any orange dye left under the sink in the kitchen. If I add water to it, I can dye Mom's blouse and it will look like new.*

Hattie waited until after dinner when no one was in the kitchen. Quickly she got out the dishpan and poured in the leftover dye. Then she added some water and Mom's blouse. Back and forth she stirred the blouse. It began to turn orange.

When she thought the color was just right, she squeezed out the extra water and wrapped it in a towel. She took it up to her room to let it dry.

Tomorrow is Mom's birthday, and I'll surprise her with her new blouse then, Hattie determined.

The following day at supper, Hattie's family sang "Happy Birthday" to Mom and then the children eagerly presented their gifts. Pierce presented her with a package of clothespins. Clarence gave her a new pair of shoestrings, and Leona and Elmer each gave her an orange.

Hattie couldn't wait for Mom to see the gift she was giving her.

"Here Mom," said Hattie, beaming. "I made this especially for you. It's not new, just different."

When Mom unwrapped the package, she nearly dropped it on the floor.

"My Sunday blouse! Oh, my! What happened, Hattie?" asked Mom in dismay.

Dad and Pierce both gasped. "Now you've gone and done it," said Pierce.

Hattie tried to explain. "I wanted you to have something sort of new for your birthday since you gave us all something new for Easter."

Mom looked at Hattie kindly. "You meant well, Hattie. Thank you."

Clarence couldn't believe his ears. "Hattie ruined your good blouse and you're thanking her for it?" he asked. "If I had done that, I'd be getting a spanking in the woodshed."

"Everybody is just making fun of me!" Hattie cried

When Mom unwrapped the package, she nearly dropped it on the floor.

and ran upstairs to her bedroom.

Mom followed her up to her room.

"I'll iron the blouse and I can still wear it," said Mom. "It's a pretty color."

"No, it's not pretty." Hattie answered. "I should have asked you if it was okay before I dyed it. I'm sorry."

"Yes, Hattie," said Mom. "That would have been a good idea. But next time, you'll know what to do."

Hattie was glad Mom wasn't angry. "Thanks for not being too mad . . . and for my new Easter dress," Hattie said.

"Ya, you're welcome," Mom replied. "I like to buy you a pretty new Easter dress better than to buy something for me. For you to say 'Thank you' is a good present for me."

Just like Jesus, thought Hattie.

Experience the *Treasures of Childhood*

Growing up in a twelve-member family on a farm in the 1920s creates many opportunities for adventure and discovery. Enjoy each exciting book in the *Treasures of Childhood* series as young Hattie Hart explores the magnificent world around her and learns important value lessons in the process.

Meet Hattie

Hattie has a difficult time obeying the simple rules on her family's farm. Whether she's stretching the truth to sell seeds or breaking Mom's best candy dish, each new day teaches her the value of her family's love.

Hattie's Faraway Family

Hattie volunteers to drive Mrs. Lynn to Worthington— even though she's never driven before. Then, baby Elmer disappears at the beach when she is suppose to be watching him. These adventures and others teach Hattie the importance of responsibility.

Hattie's Holidays

Hattie sneaks out of the house on her birthday to try out her new skates—and breaks her ankle! Then, she lights a candle and accidentally sets the Christmas tree on fire. Through these experiences, Hattie learns the hard way that rules are not to spoil her fun, but to protect her.

All titles are available at your favorite Christian bookstore.